Ann Morgan Woodward

A TEACHER ON ROLLER SKATES
and Other School Riddles

A TEACHER ON ROLLER SKATES

and Other School Riddles

by David A. Adler

illustrated by
John Wallner

Holiday House / New York

To my niece Alyse.
D.A.A.

For Stuart Klein.
Yuck, yuck, yuck.
J.C.W.

Text copyright © 1989 by David A. Adler
Illustrations copyright © 1989 by John C. Wallner
All rights reserved
Printed in the United States of America
First Edition

Library of Congress Cataloging-in-Publication Data

Adler, David A.
A teacher on roller skates and other school riddles / by David A.
Adler ; illustrated by John Wallner. — 1st ed.
p. cm.
Summary: a collection of jokes and riddles about school, including
"Should you do your homework in your pajamas? No. You should do it
in a notebook."
ISBN 0-8234-0775-6
1. Riddles, Juvenile. 2. Teachers—Juvenile humor. 3. Schools—
Juvenile humor. 4. American wit and humor, Juvenile.
[1. Schools—Wit and humor. 2. Jokes. 3. Riddles.] I. Wallner,
John C., ill. II. Title.
PN6371.5.A32297 1989
818'5402—dc19   89-1929   CIP   AC

ISBN 0-8234-0775-6

Why did the teacher's watch go "Tick, tick, tick?"

It wouldn't tock (talk) in class.

Why did Humpty Dumpty have a great fall?

He was promoted.

What did some students write on a teacher's tombstone?

"Test in peace."

Why did the first grader take his school
books to bed?

The teacher said to cover them.

Why did the dog say "meow?"

He was studying a foreign language.

What happened after the star of the school play broke his leg?

He was taken out of the cast.

Should you do your homework in your pajamas?

No. You should do it in a notebook.

What has more degrees than a roomful of teachers?

A thermometer.

Why did the teacher yell at Humpty Dumpty?

He cracked up in class.

Why was Mother Hen thrown out of school?

She used fowl (foul) language.

Why did Cinderella's team lose the volleyball game?

Their coach was a pumpkin.

What happened to the children who took the school bus home?

They had to give it back.

Who is always up on current events?

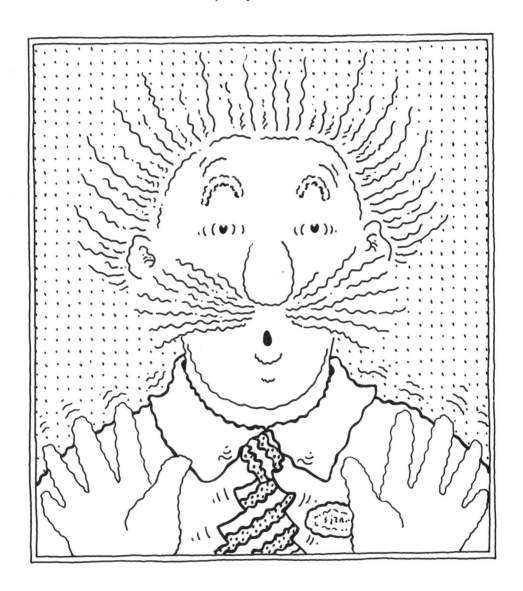

An electrician.

Why did the teacher wear sunglasses to class?

Her students were very bright.

Why are fish so smart?

They swim in schools.

When do you need goggles to read a report card?

When it's below C (sea) level.

What has twenty heads and can be very bright?

A book of matches.

What's the difference between a school bus driver and his cold?

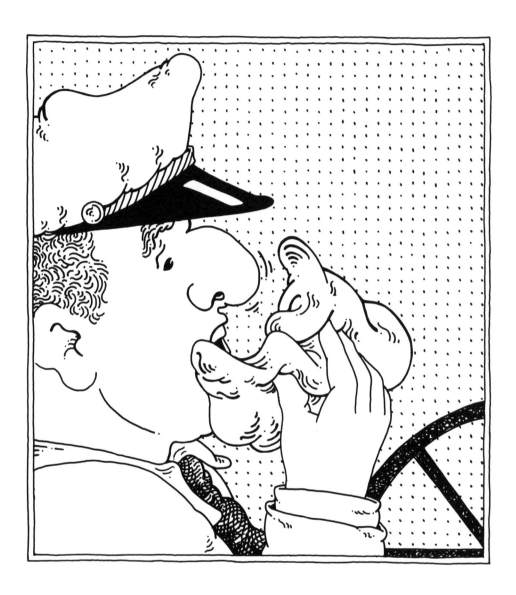

The driver knows his stops. The cold stops his nose.

Why did the owl get into trouble when the teacher called on him?

He didn't give a hoot.

What's yellow on the outside and noisy on
the inside?

A school bus.

What would you get if Dracula was your teacher?

Lots of tests—blood tests.

Why were the children eating dollar bills?

It was their lunch money.

Why was the arithmetic teacher crying?

She had too many problems.

What happened to the girl who broke the school bell?

She was awarded the no-bell (Nobel) prize.

Where would you learn to scoop ice cream?

At sundae school.

Are history teachers popular?

Sure. They always have a date.

Was the school bus driver fresh?

Yes. He told everyone where to get off.

What's the easiest way to raise your grades?

Hold your report card over your head.

Why did the music teacher keep banging his head on the piano?

He was playing by ear.

When is school the most fun?

During July and August.

Why did the teacher write on the classroom windows?

He wanted the lesson to be perfectly clear.

What has four legs and flies?

A lunchroom table.

Why did the prince take his father to school?

The teacher said "Bring a ruler."

What school did Sir Lancelot attend?

Knight (night) school.

What has seventy-two feet and sings?

The school choir.

Why did the music teacher play his trumpet alone?

He was a private tooter.

What if you crossed a principal with a frog?

Oh, no! Never cross a principal.

How do teachers learn to write on the chalkboard?

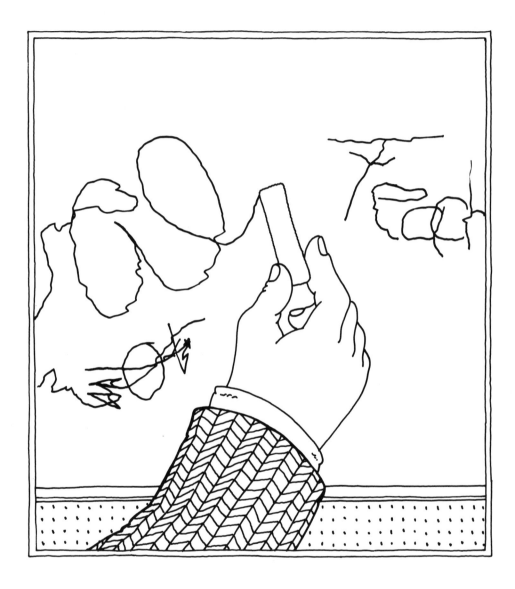

They learn from scratch.

Are bunny rabbits good in math?

**Well, they can't add, but they sure
can multiply.**

Which bus arrived long before the first day of school?

Columbus.

What smells the most in the student cafeteria?

Your nose.

Do electric eels do well in school?

Sure. They're very bright.

How is a teacher like an optometrist?

They both examine pupils.

What would you get if you crossed a cow with the class clown?

Udder (utter) nonsense.

Why did the pony stay home from school?

She was a little hoarse (horse).

Why were the Duck brothers sent out of class?

They were wise quackers.

Was Randy Reindeer promoted?

Sure. The teacher was happy to pass the buck.

Why did the math teacher call the parrot "Grandma?"

It was his polygram (Polly-gram).

What pencil is much too big to bring to school?

Pennsylvania.

Why did the raspberries meet with the school psychologist?

They were in a jam.

Why was the cross-eyed teacher fired?

He couldn't control his pupils.

How do most children like school?

Closed.

**Who has chalk on her fingers and wheels
on her feet?**

A teacher on roller skates.

What would a witch study in school?

Spelling.

Which schools have elevators?

High schools.

Why is the student cafeteria like a tennis player's luggage?

There's a racket in both.

Why did the math teacher bring rags to school?

To dust the multiplication tables.

Why was the home economics class empty?

The recipe said, "Take one egg and beat it."

What animal always gets in trouble while taking a test?

The cheetah.

What gives a math teacher more trouble than an angry triangle?

A vicious circle.